W9-AMT-841

LET'S
PLAY

For Joan

First published in 2014

Allen & Unwin
83 Alexander Street
Crows Nest NSW 2065
Australia
Phone: (61 2) 8425 0100
Email: info@allenandunwin.com
Web: www.allenandunwin.com

A Cataloguing-in-Publication entry is available
from the National Library of Australia
www.trove.nla.gov.au

ISBN 978 174331 628 3

Cover and text design by Sandra Nobes
Set in 18 pt Century Oldstyle by Sandra Nobes
This book was printed in March 2014 at Hang Tai Printing (Guang Dong) Ltd,
Xin Cheng Ind. Est., Xie Gang Town, Dong Guan, Guang Dong Province, China.

1 3 5 7 9 10 8 6 4 2

LET'S
PLAY
ALBOROZO
ALLEN&UNWIN
SYDNEY • MELBOURNE • AUCKLAND • LONDON

‘Good morning children!

Would you like to learn about the orchestra?’

'An orchestra is made up of many different instruments, and many different sounds.

So let me show you some of them.'

‘First, let’s visit the percussion section.
Here we have the timpani, or just “timps”.’

'Oh, splendid playing there, Sergio!'

'And I'm sure you all know the cymbals.'

‘Don’t bang *too* hard, Jeffery!’

'Here is the xylophone.'

‘Lovely tune there, Marguerite!’

‘In the brass section we have instruments like the trumpet and the trombone.’

'And let's not forget the tuba!

Amazing, Gerard! Stupendous sound!'

'Now we come to the strings.
These of course are the violins, violas and cello.'

'Beautiful, all of you…
just beautiful.
Children, we can meet the
double bass another day.'

'Now a tiny instrument! The piccolo.
It belongs to the woodwind section.

Heehee…that tickles, Henri!’

'And coming soon, here's the bassoon.'

‘Not to mention the other woodwinds,
oboe, clarinet and flute.’

'And now, a very important instrument that sometimes plays with the orchestra. The piano!'

'Ahhh...I can almost see the music!'

'Last we have – the harp!

Very fine fingering, Gwendoline.'

'So let's see how they all fit together, shall we?

One, two, three…'

MAGNIFICO!

CLAP
Clap
CLAP